Jack London

Stories of Ships and the Sea

weitsuechtig

Jack London

Stories of Ships and the Sea

ISBN/EAN: 9783943850741

Auflage: 1

Erscheinungsjahr: 2013

Erscheinungsort: Bremen, Deutschland

@ weitsuechtig in Access Verlag GmbH, Fahrenheitstr. 1, 28359 Bremen. Alle Rechte beim Verlag und bei den jeweiligen Lizenzgebern.

weitsuechtig

CONTENTS

CHRIS FARRINGTON: ABLE SEAMAN

"If you vas in der old country ships, a liddle shaver like you vood pe only der boy, und you vood wait on der able seamen. Und ven der able seaman sing out, 'Boy, der water-jug!' you vood jump quick, like a shot, und bring der water-jug. Und ven der able seaman sing out, 'Boy, my boots!' you vood get der boots. Und you vood pe politeful, und say 'Yessir' und 'No sir.' But you pe in der American ship, and you t'ink you are so good as der able seamen. Chris, mine boy, I haf ben a sailorman for twenty-two years, und do you t'ink you are so good as me? I vas a sailorman pefore you vas borned, und I knot und reef und splice ven you play mit topstrings und fly kites."

"But you are unfair, Emil!" cried Chris Farrington, his sensitive face flushed and hurt. He was a slender though strongly built young fellow of seventeen, with Yankee ancestry writ large all over him.

"Dere you go vonce again!" the Swedish sailor exploded. "My name is Mister Johansen, und a kid of a boy like you call me 'Emil!' It vas insulting, und comes pecause of der American ship!"

"But you call me 'Chris'!" the boy expostulated, reproachfully.

"But you vas a boy."

"Who does a man's work," Chris retorted. "And because I do a man's work I have as much right to call you by your first name as you me. We are all equals in this fo'castle, and you know it. When we signed for the voyage in San Francisco, we signed as sailors on the *Sophie Sutherland* and there was no difference made with any of us. Haven't I always done my work? Did I ever shirk? Did you or any other man ever have to take a wheel for me? Or a lookout? Or go aloft?"

"Chris is right," interrupted a young English sailor. "No man has had to do a tap of his work yet. He signed as good as any of us and he's shown himself as good — "

"Better!" broke in a Novia Scotia man. "Better than some of us! When we struck the sealing-grounds he turned out to be next to the best boat-steerer aboard. Only French Louis, who'd been at it for years, could beat him. I'm only a boat-puller, and you're only a boat-puller, too, Emil Johansen, for all your twenty-two years at sea. Why don't you become a boat-steerer?"

"Too clumsy," laughed the Englishman, "and too slow."

"Little that counts, one way or the other," joined in Dane Jurgensen, coming to the aid of his Scandinavian brother. "Emil is a man grown and an able seaman; the boy is neither."

And so the argument raged back and forth, the Swedes, Norwegians and Danes, because of race kinship, taking the part of Johansen, and the English, Canadians and Americans taking the part of Chris. From an unprejudiced point of view, the right was on the side of Chris. As he had truly said, he did a man's work, and the same work that any of them did. But they were prejudiced, and badly so, and out of the words which passed rose a standing quarrel which divided the forecastle into two parties.

The *Sophie Sutherland* was a seal-hunter, registered out of San Francisco, and engaged in hunting the furry sea-animals along the Japanese coast north to Bering Sea. The other vessels were two-masted schooners, but she was a three-master and the largest in the fleet. In fact, she was a full-rigged, three-topmast schooner, newly built.

Although Chris Farrington knew that justice was with him, and that he performed all his work faithfully and well, many a time, in secret thought, he longed for some pressing emergency to arise whereby he could demonstrate to the Scandinavian seamen that he also was an able seaman.

But one stormy night, by an accident for which he was in nowise accountable, in overhauling a spare anchor-chain he had all the fingers of his left hand badly crushed. And his hopes were likewise crushed, for it was impossible for him to continue hunting with the boats, and he was forced to stay idly aboard until his fingers should heal. Yet, although he little dreamed it, this very accident was to give him the long-looked-for-opportunity.

One afternoon in the latter part of May the *Sophie Sutherland* rolled sluggishly in a breathless calm. The seals were abundant, the hunting good, and the boats were all away and out of sight. And with them was almost every man of the crew. Besides Chris, there remained only the captain, the sailing-master and the Chinese cook.

The captain was captain only by courtesy. He was an old man, past eighty, and blissfully ignorant of the sea and its ways; but he was the owner of the vessel, and hence the honorable title. Of course the sailing-master, who was really captain, was a thorough-going seaman. The mate, whose post was aboard, was out with the boats, having temporarily taken Chris's place as boat-steerer.

When good weather and good sport came together, the boats were accustomed to range far and wide, and often did not return to the schooner until long after dark. But for all that it was a perfect hunting day, Chris noted a growing anxiety on the part of the sailing-master. He paced the deck nervously, and was constantly sweeping the horizon with his marine glasses. Not a boat was in sight. As sunset arrived, he even sent Chris aloft to the mizzen-topmast-head, but with no better luck. The boats could not possibly be back before midnight.

Since noon the barometer had been falling with startling rapidity, and all the signs were ripe for a great storm — how great, not even the sailing-master anticipated. He and Chris set to work to prepare for it. They put storm gaskets on the furled topsails, lowered and stowed the foresail and spanker and took in the two inner jibs. In the one remaining jib they put a single reef, and a single reef in the mainsail.

Night had fallen before they finished, and with the darkness came the storm. A low moan swept over the sea, and the wind struck the *Sophie Suther-land* flat. But she righted quickly, and with the sail-ing-master at the wheel, sheered her bow into within five points of the wind. Working as well as he could with his bandaged hand, and with the fee-ble aid of the Chinese cook, Chris went forward and backed the jib over to the weather side. This with the flat mainsail, left the schooner hove to.

"God help the boats! It's no gale! It's a ty-phoon!" the sailing-master shouted to Chris at eleven o'clock. "Too much canvas! Got to get two more reefs into the mainsail, and got to do it right away!" He glanced at the old captain, shivering in oilskins at the binnacle and holding on for dear life. "There's only you and I, Chris — and the cook; but he's next to worthless!"

In order to make the reef, it was necessary to lower the mainsail, and the removal of this after pressure was bound to make the schooner fall off before the wind and sea because of the forward pressure of the jib.

"Take the wheel!" the sailing-master directed. "And when I give the word, hard up with it! And when she's square before it, steady her! And keep her there! We'll heave to again as soon as I get the reefs in!"

Gripping the kicking spokes, Chris watched him and the reluctant cook go forward into the howling darkness. The *Sophie Sutherland* was plunging into the huge head-seas and wallowing tremendously, the tense steel stays and taut rigging humming like harp-strings to the wind. A buffeted cry came to his ears, and he felt the schooner's bow paying off of its own accord. The mainsail was down!

He ran the wheel hard-over and kept anxious track of the changing direction of the wind on his face and of the heave of the vessel. This was the crucial moment. In performing the evolution she would have to pass broadside to the surge before she could get before it. The wind was blowing directly on his right cheek, when he felt the *Sophie Sutherland* lean over and begin to rise toward the sky — up — up — an infinite distance! Would she clear the crest of the gigantic wave?

Again by the feel of it, for he could see nothing, he knew that a wall of water was rearing and curving far above him along the whole weather side. There was an instant's calm as the liquid wall intervened and shut off the wind. The schooner righted, and for that instant seemed at perfect rest. Then she rolled to meet the descending rush.

Chris shouted to the captain to hold tight, and prepared himself for the shock. But the man did not live who could face it. An ocean of water smote Chris's back and his clutch on the spokes was loosened as if it were a baby's. Stunned, powerless, like a straw on the face of a torrent, he was swept onward he knew not whither. Missing the corner of the cabin, he was dashed forward along the poop runway a hundred feet or more, striking violently against the foot of the foremast. A second wave, crushing inboard, hurled him back the way he had come, and left him half-drowned where the poop steps should have been.

Bruised and bleeding, dimly conscious, he felt for the rail and dragged himself to his feet. Unless something could be done, he knew the last moment had come. As he faced the poop, the wind drove into his mouth with suffocating force. This brought him back to his senses with a start. The wind was blowing from dead aft! The schooner was out of the trough and before it! But the send of the sea was bound to breach her to again. Crawling up the runway, he managed to get to the wheel just in time to prevent this. The binnacle light was still burning. They were safe!

That is, he and the schooner were safe. As to the welfare of his three companions he could not say. Nor did he dare leave the wheel in order to find out, for it took every second of his undivided attention to keep the vessel to her course. The least fraction of carelessness and the heave of the sea under the quarter was liable to thrust her into the trough. So, a boy of one hundred and forty pounds, he clung to his herculean task of guiding the two hundred straining tons of fabric amid the chaos of the great storm forces.

Half an hour later, groaning and sobbing, the captain crawled to Chris's feet. All was lost, he whimpered. He was smitten unto death. The galley had gone by the board, the mainsail and running-gear, the cook, every thing!

"Where's the sailing-master?" Chris demanded when he had caught his breath after steadying a wild lurch of the schooner. It was no child's play to steer a vessel under single reefed jib before a typhoon.

"Clean up for'ard," the old man replied "Jammed under the fo'c'sle-head, but still breathing. Both his arms are broken, he says and he doesn't know how many ribs. He's hurt bad."

"Well, he'll drown there the way she's shipping water through the hawse-pipes. Go for'ard!" Chris commanded, taking charge of things as a matter of course. "Tell him not to worry; that I'm at the wheel. Help him as much as you can, and make him help" — he stopped and ran the spokes to starboard as a tremendous billow rose under the stern and yawed the schooner to port — "and make him help himself for the rest. Unship the fo'castle hatch and get him down into a bunk. Then ship the hatch again."

The captain turned his aged face forward and wavered pitifully. The waist of the ship was full of water to the bulwarks. He had just come through it, and knew death lurked every inch of the way.

"Go!" Chris shouted, fiercely. And as the fear-stricken man started, "And take another look for the cook!"

Two hours later, almost dead from suffering, the captain returned. He had obeyed orders. The sailing-master was helpless, although safe in a bunk; the cook was gone. Chris sent the captain below to the cabin to change his clothes.

After interminable hours of toil day broke cold and gray. Chris looked about him. The *Sophie Sutherland* was racing before the typhoon like a thing possessed. There was no rain, but the wind whipped the spray of the sea mast-high, obscuring everything except in the immediate neighborhood.

Two waves only could Chris see at a time — the one before and the one behind. So small and insignificant the schooner seemed on the long Pacific roll! Rushing up a maddening mountain, she would poise like a cockle-shell on the giddy summit, breathless and rolling, leap outward and down into the yawning chasm beneath, and bury herself in the smother of foam at the bottom. Then the recovery, another mountain, another sickening upward rush, another poise, and the downward crash. Abreast of him, to starboard, like a ghost of the storm, Chris saw the cook dashing apace with the schooner. Evidently, when washed overboard, he had grasped and become entangled in a trailing halyard.

For three hours more, alone with this gruesome companion, Chris held the *Sophie Sutherland* before the wind and sea. He had long since forgotten his mangled fingers. The bandages had been torn away, and the cold, salt spray had eaten into the half-healed wounds until they were numb and no longer pained. But he was not cold. The terrific labor of steering forced the perspiration from every pore. Yet he was faint and weak with hunger and exhaustion, and hailed with delight the advent on deck of the captain, who fed him all of a pound of cake-chocolate. It strengthened him at once.

He ordered the captain to cut the halyard by which the cook's body was towing, and also to go forward and cut loose the jib-halyard and sheet. When he had done so, the jib fluttered a couple of moments like a handkerchief, then tore out of the bolt-ropes and vanished. The *Sophie Sutherland* was running under bare poles.

By noon the storm had spent itself, and by six in the evening the waves had died down sufficiently to let Chris leave the helm. It was almost hopeless to dream of the small boats weathering the typhoon, but there is always the chance in saving human life, and Chris at once applied himself to going back over the course along which he had fled. He managed to get a reef in one of the inner jibs and two reefs in the spanker, and then, with the aid of the watch-tackle, to hoist them to the stiff breeze that yet blew. And all through the night, tacking back and forth on the back track, he shook out canvas as fast as the wind would permit.

The injured sailing-master had turned delirious and between tending him and lending a hand with the ship, Chris kept the captain busy. "Taught me more seamanship," as he afterward said, "than I'd learned on the whole voyage." But by daybreak the old man's feeble frame succumbed, and he fell off into exhausted sleep on the weather poop.

Chris, who could now lash the wheel, covered the tired man with blankets from below, and went fishing in the lazaretto for something to eat. But by the day following he found himself forced to give in, drowsing fitfully by the wheel and waking ever and anon to take a look at things.

On the afternoon of the third day he picked up a schooner, dismasted and battered. As he approached, close-hauled on the wind, he saw her decks crowded by an unusually large crew, and on sailing in closer, made out among others the faces of his missing comrades. And he was just in the nick of time, for they were fighting a losing fight at the pumps. An hour later they, with the crew of the sinking craft were aboard the *Sophie Sutherland.*

Having wandered so far from their own vessel, they had taken refuge on the strange schooner just before the storm broke. She was a Canadian sealer on her first voyage, and as was now apparent, her last.

The captain of the *Sophie Sutherland* had a story to tell, also, and he told it well — so well, in fact, that when all hands were gathered together on deck during the dog-watch, Emil Johansen strode over to Chris and gripped him by the hand.

"Chris," he said, so loudly that all could hear, "Chris, I gif in. You vas yoost so good a sailorman as I. You vas a bully boy und able seaman, und I pe proud for you!

"Und Chris!" He turned as if he had forgotten something, and called back, "From dis time always you call me 'Emil' mitout der 'Mister'!"

TYPHOON OFF THE COAST OF JAPAN

Jack London's First Story, Published at the Age of Seventeen.

It was four bells in the morning watch. We had just finished breakfast when the order came forward for the watch on deck to stand by to heave her to and all hands stand by the boats.

"Port! hard a port!" cried our sailing-master. "Clew up the topsails! Let the flying jib run down! Back the jib over to windward and run down the foresail!" And so was our schooner *Sophie Sutherland* hove to off the Japan coast, near Cape Jerimo, on April 10, 1893.

Then came moments of bustle and confusion. There were eighteen men to man the six boats. Some were hooking on the falls, others casting off the lashings; boat-steerers appeared with boat-compasses and water-breakers, and boat-pullers with the lunch boxes. Hunters were staggering under two or three shotguns, a rifle and heavy ammunition box, all of which were soon stowed away with their oilskins and mittens in the boats.

The sailing-master gave his last orders, and away we went, pulling three pairs of oars to gain our positions. We were in the weather boat, and so had a longer pull than the others. The first, second and third lee boats soon had all sail set and were running off to the southward and westward with the wind beam, while the schooner was running off to leeward of them, so that in case of accident the boats would have fair wind home.

It was a glorious morning, but our boat steerer shook his head ominously as he glanced at the rising sun and prophetically muttered: "Red sun in the morning, sailor take warning." The sun had an angry look, and a few light, fleecy "nigger-heads" in that quarter seemed abashed and frightened and soon disappeared.

Away off to the northward Cape Jerimo reared its black, forbidding head like some huge monster rising from the deep. The winter's snow, not yet entirely dissipated by the sun, covered it in patches of glistening white, over which the light wind swept on its way out to sea. Huge gulls rose slowly, fluttering their wings in the light breeze and striking their webbed feet on the surface of the water for over half a mile before they could leave it. Hardly had the patter, patter died away when a flock of sea quail rose, and with whistling wings flew away to windward, where members of a large band of whales were disporting themselves, their blowings sounding like the exhaust of steam engines. The harsh, discordant cries of a sea-parrot grated unpleasantly on the ear, and set half a dozen alert in a small band of seals that were ahead of us. Away they went, breaching and jumping entirely out of water. A sea-gull with slow, deliberate flight and long, majestic curves circled round us, and as a reminder of home a little English sparrow perched impudently on the fo'castle head, and, cocking his head on one side, chirped merrily. The boats were soon among the seals, and the bang! bang! of the guns could be heard from down to leeward.

The wind was slowly rising, and by three o'clock as, with a dozen seals in our boat, we were deliberating whether to go on or turn back, the recall flag was run up at the schooner's mizzen — a sure sign that with the rising wind the barometer was falling and that our sailing-master was getting anxious for the welfare of the boats.

Away we went before the wind with a single reef in our sail. With clenched teeth sat the boat-steerer, grasping the steering oar firmly with both hands, his restless eyes on the alert — a glance at the schooner ahead, as we rose on a sea, another at the mainsheet, and then one astern where the dark ripple of the wind on the water told him of a coming puff or a large white-cap that threatened to overwhelm us. The waves were holding high carnival, performing the strangest antics, as with wild glee they danced along in fierce pursuit — now up, now down, here, there, and everywhere, until some great sea of liquid green with its milk-white crest of foam rose from the ocean's throbbing bosom and drove the others from view. But only for a moment, for again under new forms they reappeared. In the sun's path they wandered, where every ripple, great or small, every little spit or spray looked like molten silver, where the water lost its dark green color and became a dazzling, silvery flood, only to vanish and become a wild waste of sullen turbulence, each dark foreboding sea rising and breaking, then rolling on again. The dash, the sparkle, the silvery light soon vanished with the sun, which became obscured by black clouds that were rolling swiftly in from the west, northwest; apt heralds of the coming storm.

We soon reached the schooner and found our-
selves the last aboard. In a few minutes the seals
were skinned, boats and decks washed, and we
were down below by the roaring fo'castle fire, with
a wash, change of clothes, and a hot, substantial
supper before us. Sail had been put on the schooner,
as we had a run of seventy-five miles to make to the
southward before morning, so as to get in the midst
of the seals, out of which we had strayed during the
last two days' hunting.

We had the first watch from eight to midnight.
The wind was soon blowing half a gale, and our
sailing-master expected little sleep that night as he
paced up and down the poop. The topsails were
soon clewed up and made fast, then the flying jib
run down and furled. Quite a sea was rolling by this
time, occasionally breaking over the decks, flooding
them and threatening to smash the boats. At six
bells we were ordered to turn them over and put on
storm lashings. This occupied us till eight bells,
when we were relieved by the mid-watch. I was the
last to go below, doing so just as the watch on deck
was furling the spanker. Below all were asleep except our green hand, the "bricklayer," who was dying of consumption. The wildly dancing movements
of the sea lamp cast a pale, flickering light through
the fo'castle and turned to golden honey the drops
of water on the yellow oilskins. In all the corners
dark shadows seemed to come and go, while up in
the eyes of her, beyond the pall bits, descending
from deck to deck, where they seemed to lurk like
some dragon at the cavern's mouth, it was dark as
Erebus. Now and again, the light seemed to pene-

trate for a moment as the schooner rolled heavier than usual, only to recede, leaving it darker and blacker than before. The roar of the wind through the rigging came to the ear muffled like the distant rumble of a train crossing a trestle or the surf on the beach, while the loud crash of the seas on her weather bow seemed almost to rend the beams and planking asunder as it resounded through the fo'castle. The creaking and groaning of the timbers, stanchions, and bulkheads, as the strain the vessel was undergoing was felt, served to drown the groans of the dying man as he tossed uneasily in his bunk. The working of the foremast against the deck beams caused a shower of flaky powder to fall, and sent another sound mingling with the tumultuous storm. Small cascades of water streamed from the pall bits from the fo'castle head above, and, joining issue with the streams from the wet oilskins, ran along the floor and disappeared aft into the main hold.

At two bells in the middle watch — that is, in land parlance one o'clock in the morning; — the order was roared out on the fo'castle: "All hands on deck and shorten sail!"

Then the sleepy sailors tumbled out of their bunk and into their clothes, oilskins and sea-boots and up on deck. 'Tis when that order comes on cold, blustering nights that "Jack" grimly mutters: "Who would not sell a farm and go to sea?"

It was on deck that the force of the wind could be fully appreciated, especially after leaving the stifling fo'castle. It seemed to stand up against you like a wall, making it almost impossible to move on the heaving decks or to breathe as the fierce gusts came dashing by. The schooner was hove to under jib, foresail and mainsail. We proceeded to lower the foresail and make it fast. The night was dark, greatly impeding our labor. Still, though not a star or the moon could pierce the black masses of storm clouds that obscured the sky as they swept along before the gale, nature aided us in a measure. A soft light emanated from the movement of the ocean. Each mighty sea, all phosphorescent and glowing with the tiny lights of myriads of animalculae, threatened to overwhelm us with a deluge of fire. Higher and higher, thinner and thinner, the crest grew as it began to curve and overtop preparatory to breaking, until with a roar it fell over the bulwarks, a mass of soft glowing light and tons of water which sent the sailors sprawling in all directions and left in each nook and cranny little specks of light that glowed and trembled till the next sea washed them away, depositing new ones in their places. Sometimes several seas following each other with great rapidity and thundering down on our decks filled them full to the bulwarks, but soon they were discharged through the lee scuppers.

To reef the mainsail we were forced to run off before the gale under the single reefed jib. By the time we had finished the wind had forced up such a tremendous sea that it was impossible to heave her to. Away we flew on the wings of the storm through the muck and flying spray. A wind sheer to starboard, then another to port as the enormous seas struck the schooner astern and nearly broached her to. As day broke we took in the jib, leaving not a sail unfurled. Since we had begun scudding she had ceased to take the seas over her bow, but amidships they broke fast and furious. It was a dry storm in the matter of rain, but the force of the wind filled the air with fine spray, which flew as high as the crosstrees and cut the face like a knife, making it impossible to see over a hundred yards ahead. The sea was a dark lead color as with long, slow, majestic roll it was heaped up by the wind into liquid mountains of foam. The wild antics of the schooner were sickening as she forged along. She would almost stop, as though climbing a mountain, then rapidly rolling to right and left as she gained the summit of a huge sea, she steadied herself and paused for a moment as though affrighted at the yawning precipice before her. Like an avalanche, she shot forward and down as the sea astern struck her with the force of a thousand battering rams, burying her bow to the cat-heads in the milky foam at the bottom that came on deck in all directions — forward, astern, to right and left, through the hawse-pipes and over the rail.

The wind began to drop, and by ten o'clock we were talking of heaving her to. We passed a ship, two schooners and a four-masted barkentine under the smallest canvas, and at eleven o'clock, running up the spanker and jib, we hove her to, and in another hour we were beating back again against the aftersea under full sail to regain the sealing ground away to the westward.

Below, a couple of men were sewing the "bricklayer's" body in canvas preparatory to the sea burial.

And so with the storm passed away the "bricklayer's" soul.

THE LOST POACHER

"But they won't take excuses. You're across the line, and that's enough. They'll take you. In you go, Siberia and the salt mines. And as for Uncle Sam, why, what's he to know about it? Never a word will get back to the States. 'The *Mary Thomas*,' the papers will say, 'the *Mary Thomas* lost with all hands. Probably in a typhoon in the Japanese seas.' That's what the papers will say, and people, too. In you go, Siberia and the salt mines. Dead to the world and kith and kin, though you live fifty years."

In such manner John Lewis, commonly known as the "sea-lawyer," settled the matter out of hand.

It was a serious moment in the forecastle of the *Mary Thomas*. No sooner had the watch below begun to talk the trouble over, than the watch on deck came down and joined them. As there was no wind, every hand could be spared with the exception of the man at the wheel, and he remained only for the sake of discipline. Even "Bub" Russell, the cabin-boy, had crept forward to hear what was going on.

However, it was a serious moment, as the grave faces of the sailors bore witness. For the three preceding months the *Mary Thomas* sealing schooner, had hunted the seal pack along the coast of Japan and north to Bering Sea. Here, on the Asiatic side of the sea, they were forced to give over the chase, or rather, to go no farther; for beyond, the Russian cruisers patrolled forbidden ground, where the seals might breed in peace.

A week before she had fallen into a heavy fog accompanied by calm. Since then the fog-bank had not lifted, and the only wind had been light airs and catspaws. This in itself was not so bad, for the sealing schooners are never in a hurry so long as they are in the midst of the seals; but the trouble lay in the fact that the current at this point bore heavily to the north. Thus the *Mary Thomas* had unwittingly drifted across the line, and every hour she was penetrating, unwillingly, farther and farther into the dangerous waters where the Russian bear kept guard.

How far she had drifted no man knew. The sun had not been visible for a week, nor the stars, and the captain had been unable to take observations in order to determine his position. At any moment a cruiser might swoop down and hale the crew away to Siberia. The fate of other poaching seal-hunters was too well known to the men of the *Mary Thomas,* and there was cause for grave faces.

"Mine friends," spoke up a German boat-steerer, "it vas a pad piziness. Shust as ve make a big catch, und all honest, somedings go wrong, und der Russians nab us, dake our skins and our schooner, und send us mit der anarchists to Siberia. Ach! a pretty pad piziness!"

"Yes, that's where it hurts," the sea lawyer went on. "Fifteen hundred skins in the salt piles, and all honest, a big pay-day coming to every man Jack of us, and then to be captured and lose it all! It'd be different if we'd been poaching, but it's all honest work in open water."

"But if we haven't done anything wrong, they can't do anything to us, can they?" Bub queried.

"It strikes me as 'ow it ain't the proper thing for a boy o' your age shovin' in when 'is elders is talkin'," protested an English sailor, from over the edge of his bunk.

"Oh, that's all right, Jack," answered the sea-lawyer. "He's a perfect right to. Ain't he just as liable to lose his wages as the rest of us?"

"Wouldn't give thruppence for them!" Jack sniffed back. He had been planning to go home and see his family in Chelsea when he was paid off, and he was now feeling rather blue over the highly possible loss, not only of his pay, but of his liberty.

"How are they to know?" the sea-lawyer asked in answer to Bub's previous question. "Here we are in forbidden water. How do they know but what we came here of our own accord? Here we are, fifteen hundred skins in the hold. How do they know whether we got them in open water or in the closed sea? Don't you see, Bub, the evidence is all against us. If you caught a man with his pockets full of apples like those which grow on your tree, and if you caught him in your tree besides, what'd you think if he told you he couldn't help it, and had just been sort of blown there, and that anyway those apples came from some other tree — what'd you think, eh?"

Bub saw it clearly when put in that light, and shook his head despondently.

"You'd rather be dead than go to Siberia," one of the boat-pullers said. "They put you into the salt-mines and work you till you die. Never see daylight again. Why, I've heard tell of one fellow that was chained to his mate, and that mate died. And they were both chained together! And if they send you to the quicksilver mines you get salivated. I'd rather be hung than salivated."

"Wot's salivated?" Jack asked, suddenly sitting up in his bunk at the hint of fresh misfortunes.

"Why, the quicksilver gets into your blood; I think that's the way. And your gums all swell like you had the scurvy, only worse, and your teeth get loose in your jaws. And big ulcers forms, and then you die horrible. The strongest man can't last long a-mining quicksilver."

"A pad piziness," the boat-steerer reiterated, dolorously, in the silence which followed. "A pad piziness. I vish I vas in Yokohama. Eh? Vot vas dot?"

The vessel had suddenly heeled over. The decks were aslant. A tin pannikin rolled down the inclined plane, rattling and banging. From above came the slapping of canvas and the quivering rat-tat-tat of the after leech of the loosely stretched fore-sail. Then the mate's voice sang down the hatch, "All hands on deck and make sail!"

Never had such summons been answered with more enthusiasm. The calm had broken. The wind had come which was to carry them south into safety. With a wild cheer all sprang on deck. Working with mad haste, they flung out topsails, flying jibs and staysails. As they worked, the fog-bank lifted and the black vault of heaven, bespangled with the old familiar stars, rushed into view. When all was shipshape, the *Mary Thomas* was lying gallantly over on her side to a beam wind and plunging ahead due south.

"Steamer's lights ahead on the port bow, sir!" cried the lookout from his station on the forecastlehead. There was excitement in the man's voice.

The captain sent Bub below for his nightglasses. Everybody crowded to the lee-rail to gaze at the suspicious stranger, which already began to loom up vague and indistinct. In those unfrequented waters the chance was one in a thousand that it could be anything else than a Russian patrol. The captain was still anxiously gazing through the glasses, when a flash of flame left the stranger's side, followed by the loud report of a cannon. The worst fears were confirmed. It was a patrol, evidently firing across the bows of the *Mary Thomas* in order to make her heave to.

"Hard down with your helm!" the captain commanded the steersman, all the life gone out of his voice. Then to the crew, "Back over the jib and foresail! Run down the flying jib! Clew up the foretopsail! And aft here and swing on to the mainsheet!"

The *Mary Thomas* ran into the eye of the wind, lost headway, and fell to courtesying gravely to the long seas rolling up from the west.

The cruiser steamed a little nearer and lowered a boat. The sealers watched in heartbroken silence. They could see the white bulk of the boat as it was slacked away to the water, and its crew sliding aboard. They could hear the creaking of the davits and the commands of the officers. Then the boat sprang away under the impulse of the oars, and came toward them. The wind had been rising, and already the sea was too rough to permit the frail craft to lie alongside the tossing schooner; but watching their chance, and taking advantage of the boarding ropes thrown to them, an officer and a couple of men clambered aboard. The boat then sheered off into safety and lay to its oars, a young midshipman, sitting in the stern and holding the yoke-lines, in charge.

The officer, whose uniform disclosed his rank as that of second lieutenant in the Russian navy went below with the captain of the *Mary Thomas* to look at the ship's papers. A few minutes later he emerged, and upon his sailors removing the hatch-covers, passed down into the hold with a lantern to inspect the salt piles. It was a goodly heap which confronted him — fifteen hundred fresh skins, the season's catch; and under the circumstances he could have had but one conclusion.

"I am very sorry," he said, in broken English to the sealing captain, when he again came on deck, "but it is my duty, in the name of the tsar, to seize your vessel as a poacher caught with fresh skins in the closed sea. The penalty, as you may know, is confiscation and imprisonment."

The captain of the *Mary Thomas* shrugged his shoulders in seeming indifference, and turned away. Although they may restrain all outward show, strong men, under unmerited misfortune, are sometimes very close to tears. Just then the vision of his little California home, and of the wife and two yellow-haired boys, was strong upon him, and there was a strange, choking sensation in his throat, which made him afraid that if he attempted to speak he would sob instead.

And also there was upon him the duty he owed his men. No weakness before them, for he must be a tower of strength to sustain them in misfortune. He had already explained to the second lieutenant, and knew the hopelessness of the situation. As the sea-lawyer had said, the evidence was all against him. So he turned aft, and fell to pacing up and down the poop of the vessel over which he was no longer commander.

The Russian officer now took temporary charge. He ordered more of his men aboard, and had all the canvas clewed up and furled snugly away. While this was being done, the boat plied back and forth between the two vessels, passing a heavy hawser, which was made fast to the great towing-bitts on the schooner's forecastle-head. During all this work the sealers stood about in sullen groups. It was madness to think of resisting, with the guns of a man-of-war not a biscuit-toss away; but they refused to lend a hand, preferring instead to maintain a gloomy silence.

Having accomplished his task, the lieutenant ordered all but four of his men back into the boat. Then the midshipman, a lad of sixteen, looking strangely mature and dignified in his uniform and sword, came aboard to take command of the captured sealer. Just as the lieutenant prepared to depart his eye chanced to alight upon Bub. Without a word of warning, he seized him by the arm and dropped him over the rail into the waiting boat; and then, with a parting wave of his hand, he followed him.

It was only natural that Bub should be frightened at this unexpected happening. All the terrible stories he had heard of the Russians served to make him fear them, and now returned to his mind with double force. To be captured by them was bad enough, but to be carried off by them, away from his comrades, was a fate of which he had not dreamed.

"Be a good boy, Bub," the captain called to him, as the boat drew away from the *Mary Thomas's* side, "and tell the truth!"

"Aye, aye, sir!" he answered, bravely enough by all outward appearance. He felt a certain pride of race, and was ashamed to be a coward before these strange enemies, these wild Russian bears.

"Und be politeful!" the German boat-steerer added, his rough voice lifting across the water like a fog-horn.

Bub waved his hand in farewell, and his mates clustered along the rail as they answered with a cheering shout. He found room in the stern-sheets, where he fell to regarding the lieutenant. He didn't look so wild or bearish after all — very much like other men, Bub concluded, and the sailors were much the same as all other man-of-war's men he had ever known. Nevertheless, as his feet struck the steel deck of the cruiser, he felt as if he had entered the portals of a prison.

For a few minutes he was left unheeded. The sailors hoisted the boat up, and swung it in on the davits. Then great clouds of black smoke poured out of the funnels, and they were under way — to Siberia, Bub could not help but think. He saw the *Mary Thomas* swing abruptly into line as she took the pressure from the hawser, and her side-lights, red and green, rose and fell as she was towed through the sea.

Bub's eyes dimmed at the melancholy sight, but — but just then the lieutenant came to take him down to the commander, and he straightened up and set his lips firmly, as if this were a very commonplace affair and he were used to being sent to Siberia every day in the week. The cabin in which the commander sat was like a palace compared to the humble fittings of the *Mary Thomas*, and the commander himself, in gold lace and dignity, was a most august personage, quite unlike the simple man who navigated his schooner on the trail of the seal pack.

Bub now quickly learned why he had been brought aboard, and in the prolonged questioning which followed, told nothing but the plain truth.

The truth was harmless; only a lie could have injured his cause. He did not know much, except that they had been sealing far to the south in open water, and that when the calm and fog came down upon them, being close to the line, they had drifted across. Again and again he insisted that they had not lowered a boat or shot a seal in the week they had been drifting about in the forbidden sea; but the commander chose to consider all that he said to be a tissue of falsehoods, and adopted a bullying tone in an effort to frighten the boy. He threatened and cajoled by turns, but failed in the slightest to shake Bub's statements, and at last ordered him out of his presence.

By some oversight, Bub was not put in anybody's charge, and wandered up on deck unobserved. Sometimes the sailors, in passing, bent curious glances upon him, but otherwise he was left strictly alone. Nor could he have attracted much attention, for he was small, the night dark, and the watch on deck intent on its own business. Stumbling over the strange decks, he made his way aft where he could look upon the side-lights of the *Mary Thomas*, following steadily in the rear.

For a long while he watched, and then lay down in the darkness close to where the hawser passed over the stern to the captured schooner. Once an officer came up and examined the straining rope to see if it were chafing, but Bub cowered away in the shadow undiscovered. This, however, gave him an idea which concerned the lives and liberties of twenty-two men, and which was to avert crushing sorrow from more than one happy home many thousand miles away.

In the first place, he reasoned, the crew were all guiltless of any crime, and yet were being carried relentlessly away to imprisonment in Siberia — a living death, he had heard, and he believed it implicitly. In the second place, he was a prisoner, hard and fast, with no chance to escape. In the third, it was possible for the twenty-two men on the *Mary Thomas* to escape. The only thing which bound them was a four-inch hawser. They dared not cut it at their end, for a watch was sure to be maintained upon it by their Russian captors; but at this end, ah! at his end —

Bub did not stop to reason further. Wriggling close to the hawser, he opened his jack-knife and went to work. The blade was not very sharp, and he sawed away, rope-yarn by rope-yarn, the awful picture of the solitary Siberian exile he must endure growing clearer and more terrible at every stroke. Such a fate was bad enough to undergo with one's comrades, but to face it alone seemed frightful. And besides, the very act he was performing was sure to bring greater punishment upon him.

In the midst of such somber thoughts, he heard footsteps approaching. He wriggled away into the shadow. An officer stopped where he had been working, half-stooped to examine the hawser, then changed his mind and straightened up. For a few minutes he stood there, gazing at the lights of the captured schooner, and then went forward again.

Now was the time! Bub crept back and went on sawing. Now two parts were severed. Now three. But one remained. The tension upon this was so great that it readily yielded. Splash the freed end went overboard. He lay quietly, his heart in his mouth, listening. No one on the cruiser but himself had heard.

He saw the red and green lights of the *Mary Thomas* grow dimmer and dimmer. Then a faint hallo came over the water from the Russian prize crew. Still nobody heard. The smoke continued to pour out of the cruiser's funnels, and her propellers throbbed as mightily as ever.

What was happening on the *Mary Thomas*? Bub could only surmise; but of one thing he was certain: his comrades would assert themselves and over-power the four sailors and the midshipman. A few minutes later he saw a small flash, and straining his ears heard the very faint report of a pistol. Then, oh joy! both the red and green lights suddenly disap-peared. The *Mary Thomas* was retaken!

Just as an officer came aft, Bub crept forward, and hid away in one of the boats. Not an instant too soon. The alarm was given. Loud voices rose in command. The cruiser altered her course. An elec-tric search-light began to throw its white rays across the sea, here, there, everywhere; but in its flashing path no tossing schooner was revealed.

Bub went to sleep soon after that, nor did he wake till the gray of dawn. The engines were puls-ing monotonously, and the water, splashing noisily, told him the decks were being washed down. One sweeping glance, and he saw that they were alone on the expanse of ocean. The *Mary Thomas* had escaped. As he lifted his head, a roar of laughter went up from the sailors. Even the officer, who ordered him taken below and locked up, could not quite conceal the laughter in his eyes. Bub thought often in the days of confinement which followed that they were not very angry with him for what he had done.

He was not far from right. There is a certain innate nobility deep down in the hearts of all men, which forces them to admire a brave act, even if it is performed by an enemy. The Russians were in nowise different from other men. True, a boy had outwitted them; but they could not blame him, and they were sore puzzled as to what to do with him. It would never do to take a little mite like him in to represent all that remained of the lost poacher.

So, two weeks later, a United States man-of-war, steaming out of the Russian port of Vladivostok, was signaled by a Russian cruiser. A boat passed between the two ships, and a small boy dropped over the rail upon the deck of the American vessel. A week later he was put ashore at Hakodate, and after some telegraphing, his fare was paid on the railroad to Yokohama.

From the depot he hurried through the quaint Japanese streets to the harbor, and hired a sampan boatman to put him aboard a certain vessel whose familiar rigging had quickly caught his eye. Her gaskets were off, her sails unfurled; she was just starting back to the United States. As he came closer, a crowd of sailors sprang upon the forecastle head, and the windlass-bars rose and fell as the anchor was torn from its muddy bottom.

"'Yankee ship come down the ribber!'" the sea-lawyer's voice rolled out as he led the anchor song.

"Pull, my bully boys, pull!'" roared back the old familiar chorus, the men's bodies lifting and bending to the rhythm.

Bub Russell paid the boatman and stepped on deck. The anchor was forgotten. A mighty cheer went up from the men, and almost before he could catch his breath he was on the shoulders of the captain, surrounded by his mates, and endeavoring to answer twenty questions to the second.

The next day a schooner hove to off a Japanese fishing village, sent ashore four sailors and a little midshipman, and sailed away. These men did not talk English, but they had money and quickly made their way to Yokohama. From that day the Japanese village folk never heard anything more about them, and they are still a much-talked-of mystery. As the Russian government never said anything about the incident, the United States is still ignorant of the whereabouts of the lost poacher, nor has she ever heard, officially, of the way in which some of her citizens "shanghaied" five subjects of the tsar. Even nations have secrets sometimes.

THE BANKS OF THE SACRAMENTO

> *"And it's blow, ye winds, heigh-ho,*
> *For Cal-i-for-ni-o;*
> *For there's plenty of gold so I've been told,*
> *On the banks of the Sacramento!"*

It was only a little boy, singing in a shrill treble the sea chantey which seamen sing the wide world over when they man the capstan bars and break the anchors out for "Frisco" port. It was only a little boy who had never seen the sea, but two hundred feet beneath him rolled the Sacramento. "Young" Jerry he was called, after "Old" Jerry, his father, from whom he had learned the song, as well as received his shock of bright-red hair, his blue, dancing eyes, and his fair and inevitably freckled skin.

For Old Jerry had been a sailor, and had followed the sea till middle life, haunted always by the words of the ringing chantey. Then one day he had sung the song in earnest, in an Asiatic port, swinging and thrilling round the capstan-circle with twenty others. And at San Francisco he turned his back upon his ship and upon the sea, and went to behold with his own eyes the banks of the Sacramento.

He beheld the gold, too, for he found employment at the Yellow Dream mine, and proved of utmost usefulness in rigging the great ore-cables across the river and two hundred feet above its surface.

After that he took charge of the cables and kept them in repair, and ran them and loved them, and became himself an indispensable fixture of the Yellow Dream mine. Then he loved pretty Margaret Kelly; but she had left him and Young Jerry, the latter barely toddling, to take up her last long sleep in the little graveyard among the great sober pines.

Old Jerry never went back to the sea. He remained by his cables, and lavished upon them and Young Jerry all the love of his nature. When evil days came to the Yellow Dream, he still remained in the employ of the company as watchman over the all but abandoned property.

But this morning he was not visible. Young Jerry only was to be seen, sitting on the cabin step and singing the ancient chantey. He had cooked and eaten his breakfast all by himself, and had just come out to take a look at the world. Twenty feet before him stood the steel drum round which the endless cable worked. By the drum, snug and fast, was the ore-car. Following with his eyes the dizzy flight of the cables to the farther bank, he could see the other drum and the other car.

The contrivance was worked by gravity, the loaded car crossing the river by virtue of its own weight, and at the same time dragging the empty car back. The loaded car being emptied, and the empty car being loaded with more ore, the performance could be repeated — a performance which had been repeated tens of thousands of times since the day Old Jerry became the keeper of the cables.

Young Jerry broke off his song at the sound of approaching footsteps. A tall, blue-shirted man, a rifle across the hollow of his arm, came out from the gloom of the pine-trees. It was Hall, watchman of the Yellow Dragon mine, the cables of which spanned the Sacramento a mile farther up.

"Yello, younker!" was his greeting. "What you doin' here by your lonesome?"

"Oh, bachin'," Jerry tried to answer unconcernedly, as if it were a very ordinary sort of thing. "Dad's away, you see."

"Where's he gone?" the man asked.

"San Francisco. Went last night. His brother's dead in the old country, and he's gone down to see the lawyers. Won't be back till tomorrow night."

So spoke Jerry, and with pride, because of the responsibility which had fallen to him of keeping an eye on the property of the Yellow Dream, and the glorious adventure of living alone on the cliff above the river and of cooking his own meals.

"Well, take care of yourself," Hall said, "and don't monkey with the cables. I'm goin' to see if I can pick up a deer in the Cripple Cow Cañon."

"It's goin' to rain, I think," Jerry said, with mature deliberation.

"And it's little I mind a wettin'," Hall laughed, as he strode away among the trees.

Jerry's prediction concerning rain was more than fulfilled. By ten o'clock the pines were swaying and moaning, the cabin windows rattling, and the rain driving by in fierce squalls. At half past eleven he kindled a fire, and promptly at the stroke of twelve sat down to his dinner.

No out-of-doors for him that day, he decided, when he had washed the few dishes and put them neatly away; and he wondered how wet Hall was and whether he had succeeded in picking up a deer.

At one o'clock there came a knock at the door, and when he opened it a man and a woman staggered in on the breast of a great gust of wind. They were Mr. and Mrs. Spillane, ranchers, who lived in a lonely valley a dozen miles back from the river.

"Where's Hall?" was Spillane's opening speech, and he spoke sharply and quickly.

Jerry noted that he was nervous and abrupt in his movements, and that Mrs. Spillane seemed laboring under some strong anxiety. She was a thin, washed-out, worked-out woman, whose life of dreary and unending toil had stamped itself harshly upon her face. It was the same life that had bowed her husband's shoulders and gnarled his hands and turned his hair to a dry and dusty gray.

"He's gone hunting up Cripple Cow," Jerry answered. "Did you want to cross?"

The woman began to weep quietly, while Spillane dropped a troubled exclamation and strode to the window. Jerry joined him in gazing out to where the cables lost themselves in the thick downpour.

It was the custom of the backwoods people in that section of country to cross the Sacramento on the Yellow Dragon cable. For this service a small toll was charged, which tolls the Yellow Dragon Company applied to the payment of Hall's wages.

"We've got to get across, Jerry," Spillane said, at the same time jerking his thumb over his shoulder in the direction of his wife. "Her father's hurt at the Clover Leaf. Powder explosion. Not expected to live. We just got word."

Jerry felt himself fluttering inwardly. He knew that Spillane wanted to cross on the Yellow Dream cable, and in the absence of his father he felt that he dared not assume such a responsibility, for the cable had never been used for passengers; in fact, had not been used at all for a long time.

"Maybe Hall will be back soon," he said.

Spillane shook his head, and demanded, "Where's your father?"

"San Francisco," Jerry answered, briefly.

Spillane groaned, and fiercely drove his clenched fist into the palm of the other hand. His wife was crying more audibly, and Jerry could hear her murmuring, "And daddy's dyin', dyin'!"

The tears welled up in his own eyes, and he stood irresolute, not knowing what he should do. But the man decided for him.

"Look here, kid," he said, with determination, "the wife and me are goin' over on this here cable of yours! Will you run it for us?"

Jerry backed slightly away. He did it unconsciously, as if recoiling instinctively from something unwelcome.

"Better see if Hall's back," he suggested.

"And if he ain't?"

Again Jerry hesitated.

"I'll stand for the risk," Spillane added. "Don't you see, kid, we've simply got to cross!"

Jerry nodded his head reluctantly.

"And there ain't no use waitin' for Hall," Spillane went on. "You know as well as me he ain't back from Cripple Cow this time of day! So come along and let's get started."

No wonder that Mrs. Spillane seemed terrified as they helped her into the ore-car — so Jerry thought, as he gazed into the apparently fathomless gulf beneath her. For it was so filled with rain and cloud, hurtling and curling in the fierce blast, that the other shore, seven hundred feet away, was invisible, while the cliff at their feet dropped sheer down and lost itself in the swirling vapor. By all appearances it might be a mile to bottom instead of two hundred feet.

"All ready?" he asked.

"Let her go!" Spillane shouted, to make himself heard above the roar of the wind.

He had clambered in beside his wife, and was holding one of her hands in his.

Jerry looked upon this with disapproval. "You'll need all your hands for holdin' on, the way the wind's yowlin'."

The man and the woman shifted their hands accordingly, tightly gripping the sides of the car, and Jerry slowly and carefully released the brake. The drum began to revolve as the endless cable passed round it, and the car slid slowly out into the chasm, its trolley wheels rolling on the stationary cable overhead, to which it was suspended.

It was not the first time Jerry had worked the cable, but it was the first time he had done so away from the supervising eye of his father. By means of the brake he regulated the speed of the car. It needed regulating, for at times, caught by the stronger gusts of wind, it swayed violently back and forth; and once, just before it was swallowed up in a rain squall, it seemed about to spill out its human contents.

After that Jerry had no way of knowing where the car was except by means of the cable. This he watched keenly as it glided around the drum. "Three hundred feet," he breathed to himself, as the cable markings went by, "three hundred and fifty, four hundred; four hundred and — — "

The cable had stopped. Jerry threw off the brake, but it did not move. He caught the cable with his hands and tried to start it by tugging smartly. Something had gone wrong. What? He could not guess; he could not see. Looking up, he could vaguely make out the empty car, which had been crossing from the opposite cliff at a speed equal to that of the loaded car. It was about two hundred and fifty feet away. That meant, he knew, that somewhere in the gray obscurity, two hundred feet above the river and two hundred and fifty feet from the other bank, Spillane and his wife were suspended and stationary.

Three times Jerry shouted with all the shrill force of his lungs, but no answering cry came out of the storm. It was impossible for him to hear them or to make himself heard. As he stood for a moment, thinking rapidly, the flying clouds seemed to thin and lift. He caught a brief glimpse of the swollen Sacramento beneath, and a briefer glimpse of the car and the man and woman. Then the clouds descended thicker than ever.

The boy examined the drum closely, and found nothing the matter with it. Evidently it was the drum on the other side that had gone wrong. He was appalled at the thought of the man and woman out there in the midst of the storm, hanging over the abyss, rocking back and forth in the frail car and ignorant of what was taking place on shore. And he did not like to think of their hanging there while he went round by the Yellow Dragon cable to the other drum.

But he remembered a block and tackle in the tool-house, and ran and brought it. They were double blocks, and he murmured aloud, "A purchase of four," as he made the tackle fast to the endless cable. Then he heaved upon it, heaved until it seemed that his arms were being drawn out from their sockets and that his shoulder muscles would be ripped asunder. Yet the cable did not budge. Nothing remained but to cross over to the other side.

He was already soaking wet, so he did not mind the rain as he ran over the trail to the Yellow Dragon. The storm was with him, and it was easy going, although there was no Hall at the other end of it to man the brake for him and regulate the speed of the car. This he did for himself, however, by means of a stout rope, which he passed, with a turn, round the stationary cable.

As the full force of the wind struck him in mid-air, swaying the cable and whistling and roaring past it, and rocking and careening the car, he appreciated more fully what must be the condition of mind of Spillane and his wife. And this appreciation gave strength to him, as, safely across, he fought his way up the other bank, in the teeth of the gale, to the Yellow Dream cable.

To his consternation, he found the drum in thorough working order. Everything was running smoothly at both ends. Where was the hitch? In the middle, without a doubt.

From this side, the car containing Spillane was only two hundred and fifty feet away. He could make out the man and woman through the whirling vapor, crouching in the bottom of the car and exposed to the pelting rain and the full fury of the wind. In a lull between the squalls he shouted to Spillane to examine the trolley of the car.

Spillane heard, for he saw him rise up cautiously on his knees, and with his hands go over both trolley-wheels. Then he turned his face toward the bank.

"She's all right, kid!"

Jerry heard the words, faint and far, as from a remote distance. Then what was the matter? Nothing remained but the other and empty car, which he could not see, but which he knew to be there, somewhere in that terrible gulf two hundred feet beyond Spillane's car.

His mind was made up on the instant. He was only fourteen years old, slightly and wirily built; but his life had been lived among the mountains, his father had taught him no small measure of "sailoring," and he was not particularly afraid of heights.

In the tool-box by the drum he found an old monkey-wrench and a short bar of iron, also a coil of fairly new Manila rope. He looked in vain for a piece of board with which to rig a "boatswain's chair." There was nothing at hand but large planks, which he had no means of sawing, so he was compelled to do without the more comfortable form of saddle.

The saddle he rigged was very simple. With the rope he made merely a large loop round the stationary cable, to which hung the empty car. When he sat in the loop his hands could just reach the cable conveniently, and where the rope was likely to fray against the cable he lashed his coat, in lieu of the old sack he would have used had he been able to find one.

These preparations swiftly completed, he swung out over the chasm, sitting in the rope saddle and pulling himself along the cable by his hands. With him he carried the monkey-wrench and short iron bar and a few spare feet of rope. It was a slightly up-hill pull, but this he did not mind so much as the wind. When the furious gusts hurled him back and forth, sometimes half twisting him about, and he gazed down into the gray depths, he was aware that he was afraid. It was an old cable. What if it should break under his weight and the pressure of the wind?

It was fear he was experiencing, honest fear, and he knew that there was a "gone" feeling in the pit of his stomach, and a trembling of the knees which he could not quell.

But he held himself bravely to the task. The cable was old and worn, sharp pieces of wire projected from it, and his hands were cut and bleeding by the time he took his first rest, and held a shouted conversation with Spillane. The car was directly beneath him and only a few feet away, so he was able to explain the condition of affairs and his errand.

"Wish I could help you," Spillane shouted at him as he started on, "but the wife's gone all to pieces! Anyway, kid, take care of yourself! I got myself in this fix, but it's up to you to get me out!"

"Oh, I'll do it!" Jerry shouted back. "Tell Mrs. Spillane that she'll be ashore now in a jiffy!"

In the midst of pelting rain, which half-blinded him, swinging from side to side like a rapid and er-

ratic pendulum, his torn hands paining him se-
verely and his lungs panting from his exertions and
panting from the very air which the wind sometimes blew into his mouth with strangling force, he
finally arrived at the empty car.

A single glance showed him that he had not
made the dangerous journey in vain. The front trolley-wheel, loose from long wear, had jumped the
cable, and the cable was now jammed tightly between the wheel and the sheave-block.

One thing was clear — the wheel must be removed from the block. A second thing was equally
clear — while the wheel was being removed the car
would have to be fastened to the cable by the rope
he had brought.

At the end of a quarter of an hour, beyond
making the car secure, he had accomplished nothing. The key which bound the wheel on its axle was
rusted and jammed. He hammered at it with one
hand and held on the best he could with the other,
but the wind persisted in swinging and twisting his
body, and made his blows miss more often than not.
Nine-tenths of the strength he expended was in try-
ing to hold himself steady. For fear that he might
drop the monkey-wrench he made it fast to his wrist
with his handkerchief.

At the end of half an hour Jerry had hammered
the key clear, but he could not draw it out. A dozen
times it seemed that he must give up in despair, that
all the danger and toil he had gone through were for
nothing. Then an idea came to him, and he went

through his pockets with feverish haste, and found what he sought — a ten-penny nail.

But for that nail, put in his pocket he knew not when or why, he would have had to make another trip over the cable and back. Thrusting the nail through the looped head of the key, he at last had a grip, and in no time the key was out.

Then came punching and prying with the iron bar to get the wheel itself free from where it was jammed by the cable against the side of the block. After that Jerry replaced the wheel, and by means of the rope, heaved up on the car till the trolley once more rested properly on the cable.

All this took time. More than an hour and a half had elapsed since his arrival at the empty car. And now, for the first time, he dropped out of his saddle and down into the car. He removed the detaining ropes, and the trolley-wheel began slowly to revolve. The car was moving, and he knew that somewhere beyond, although he could not see, the car of Spillane was likewise moving, and in the opposite direction.

There was no need for a brake, for his weight sufficiently counterbalanced the weight in the other car; and soon he saw the cliff rising out of the cloud depths and the old familiar drum going round and round.

Jerry climbed out and made the car securely fast. He did it deliberately and carefully, and then, quite unhero-like, he sank down by the drum, regardless of the pelting storm, and burst out sobbing.

There were many reasons why he sobbed —
partly from the pain of his hand, which was excru-
ciating; partly from exhaustion; partly from relief
and release from the nerve-tension he had been under for so long; and in a large measure for thankful-
ness that the man and woman were saved.

They were not there to thank him; but somewhere beyond that howling, storm-driven gulf he
knew they were hurrying over the trail toward the
Clover Leaf.

Jerry staggered to the cabin, and his hand left
the white knob red with blood as he opened the
door, but he took no notice of it.

He was too proudly contented with himself, for
he was certain that he had done well, and he was
honest enough to admit to himself that he had done
well. But a small regret arose and persisted in his
thoughts — if his father had only been there to see!

IN YEDDO BAY

Somewhere along Theater Street he had lost it. He remembered being hustled somewhat roughly on the bridge over one of the canals that cross that busy thoroughfare. Possibly some slant-eyed, light-fingered pickpocket was even then enjoying the fifty-odd yen his purse had contained. And then again, he thought, he might have lost it himself, just lost it carelessly.

Hopelessly, and for the twentieth time, he searched in all his pockets for the missing purse. It was not there. His hand lingered in his empty hip-pocket, and he woefully regarded the voluble and vociferous restaurant-keeper, who insanely clamored: "Twenty-five sen! You pay now! Twenty-five sen!"

"But my purse!" the boy said. "I tell you I've lost it somewhere."

Whereupon the restaurant-keeper lifted his arms indignantly and shrieked: "Twenty-five sen! Twenty-five sen! You pay now!"

Quite a crowd had collected, and it was growing embarrassing for Alf Davis.

It was so ridiculous and petty, Alf thought. Such a disturbance about nothing! And, decidedly, he must be doing something. Thoughts of diving wildly through that forest of legs, and of striking out at whomsoever opposed him, flashed through his mind; but, as though divining his purpose, one of the waiters, a short and chunky chap with an evil-looking cast in one eye, seized him by the arm.

"You pay now! You pay now! Twenty-five sen!" yelled the proprietor, hoarse with rage.

Alf was red in the face, too, from mortification; but he resolutely set out on another exploration. He had given up the purse, pinning his last hope on stray coins. In the little change-pocket of his coat he found a ten-sen piece and five-copper sen; and re-membering having recently missed a ten-sen piece, he cut the seam of the pocket and resurrected the coin from the depths of the lining. Twenty-five sen he held in his hand, the sum required to pay for the supper he had eaten. He turned them over to the proprietor, who counted them, grew suddenly calm, and bowed obsequiously — in fact, the whole crowd bowed obsequiously and melted away.

Alf Davis was a young sailor, just turned six-teen, on board the *Annie Mine*, an American sailing-schooner, which had run into Yokohama to ship its season's catch of skins to London. And in this, his second trip ashore, he was beginning to snatch his first puzzling glimpses of the Oriental mind. He laughed when the bowing and kotowing was over, and turned on his heel to confront another problem. How was he to get aboard ship? It was eleven o'clock at night, and there would be no ship's boats ashore, while the outlook for hiring a native boat-man, with nothing but empty pockets to draw upon, was not particularly inviting.

Keeping a sharp lookout for shipmates, he went down to the pier. At Yokohama there are no long lines of wharves. The shipping lies out at anchor, enabling a few hundred of the short-legged people to make a livelihood by carrying passengers to and from the shore.

A dozen sampan men and boys hailed Alf and offered their services. He selected the most favorable-looking one, an old and beneficent-appearing man with a withered leg. Alf stepped into his sampan and sat down. It was quite dark and he could not see what the old fellow was doing, though he evidently was doing nothing about shoving off and getting under way. At last he limped over and peered into Alf's face.

"Ten sen," he said.

"Yes, I know, ten sen," Alf answered carelessly. "But hurry up. American schooner."

"Ten sen. You pay now," the old fellow insisted.

Alf felt himself grow hot all over at the hateful words "pay now." "You take me to American schooner; then I pay," he said.

But the man stood up patiently before him, held out his hand, and said, "Ten sen. You pay now."

Alf tried to explain. He had no money. He had lost his purse. But he would pay. As soon as he got aboard the American schooner, then he would pay. No; he would not even go aboard the American schooner. He would call to his shipmates, and they would give the sampan man the ten sen first. After that he would go aboard. So it was all right, of course.

To all of which the beneficent-appearing old man replied: "You pay now. Ten sen." And, to make matters worse, the other sampan men squatted on the pier steps, listening.

Alf, chagrined and angry, stood up to step ashore. But the old fellow laid a detaining hand on his sleeve. "You give shirt now. I take you 'Merican schooner," he proposed.

Then it was that all of Alf's American independence flamed up in his breast. The Anglo-Saxon has a born dislike of being imposed upon, and to Alf this was sheer robbery! Ten sen was equivalent to six American cents, while his shirt, which was of good quality and was new, had cost him two dollars.

He turned his back on the man without a word, and went out to the end of the pier, the crowd, laughing with great gusto, following at his heels. The majority of them were heavy-set, muscular fellows, and the July night being one of sweltering heat, they were clad in the least possible raiment. The water-people of any race are rough and turbulent, and it struck Alf that to be out at midnight on a pier-end with such a crowd of wharfmen, in a big Japanese city, was not as safe as it might be.

One burly fellow, with a shock of black hair and ferocious eyes, came up. The rest shoved in after him to take part in the discussion.

"Give me shoes," the man said. "Give me shoes now. I take you 'Merican schooner."

Alf shook his head, whereat the crowd clamored that he accept the proposal. Now the Anglo-Saxon is so constituted that to browbeat or bully him is the last way under the sun of getting him to do any certain thing. He will dare willingly, but he will not permit himself to be driven. So this attempt of the boatmen to force Alf only aroused all the dogged stubbornness of his race. The same qualities were in him that are in men who lead forlorn hopes; and there, under the stars, on the lonely pier, encircled by the jostling and shouldering gang, he resolved that he would die rather than submit to the indignity of being robbed of a single stitch of clothing. Not value, but principle, was at stake.

Then somebody thrust roughly against him from behind. He whirled about with flashing eyes, and the circle involuntarily gave ground. But the crowd was growing more boisterous. Each and every article of clothing he had on was demanded by one or another, and these demands were shouted simultaneously at the tops of very healthy lungs.

Alf had long since ceased to say anything, but he knew that the situation was getting dangerous, and that the only thing left to him was to get away. His face was set doggedly, his eyes glinted like points of steel, and his body was firmly and confidently poised. This air of determination sufficiently impressed the boatmen to make them give way before him When he started to walk toward the shore-end of the pier. But they trooped along beside more noisily than ever. One of the youngsters about Alf's size and build, impudently snatched his cap from his head; and before he could put it on his own head, Alf struck out from the shoulder, and sent the fellow rolling on the stones.

The cap flew out of his hand and disappeared among the many legs. Alf did some quick thinking, his sailor pride would not permit him to leave the cap in their hands. He followed in the direction it had sped, and soon found it under the bare foot of a stalwart fellow, who kept his weight stolidly upon it. Alf tried to get the cap by a sudden jerk, but failed. He shoved against the man's leg, but the man only grunted. It was challenge direct, and Alf accepted it. Like a flash one leg was behind the man and Alf had thrust strongly with his shoulder against the fellow's chest. Nothing could save the man from the fierce vigorousness of the trick, and he was hurled over and backward.

Next, the cap was on Alf's head and his fists were up before him. Then he whirled about to prevent attack from behind, and all those in that quarter fled precipitately. This was what he wanted. None remained between him and the shore end. The pier was narrow. Facing them and threatening with his fist those who attempted to pass him on either side, he continued his retreat. It was exciting work, walking backward and at the same time checking that surging mass of men. But the dark-skinned peoples, the world over, have learned to respect the white man's fist; and it was the battles fought by many sailors, more than his own warlike front, that gave Alf the victory.

Where the pier adjoins the shore was the station of the harbor police, and Alf backed into the electric-lighted office, very much to the amusement of the dapper lieutenant in charge. The sampan men, grown quiet and orderly, clustered like flies by the open door, through which they could see and hear what passed.

Alf explained his difficulty in few words, and demanded, as the privilege of a stranger in a strange land, that the lieutenant put him aboard in the police-boat. The lieutenant, in turn, who knew all the "rules and regulations" by heart, explained that the harbor police were not ferrymen, and that the police-boats had other functions to perform than that of transporting belated and penniless sailormen to their ships. He also said he knew the sampan men to be natural-born robbers, but that so long as they robbed within the law he was powerless. It was their right to collect fares in advance, and who was he to command them to take a passenger and collect fare at the journey's end? Alf acknowledged the justice of his remarks, but suggested that while he could not command he might persuade. The lieutenant was willing to oblige, and went to the door, from where he delivered a speech to the crowd. But they, too, knew their rights, and, when the officer had finished, shouted in chorus their abominable "Ten sen! You pay now! You pay now!"

"You see, I can do nothing," said the lieutenant, who, by the way, spoke perfect English. "But I have warned them not to harm or molest you, so you will be safe, at least. The night is warm and half over. Lie down somewhere and go to sleep. I would permit

you to sleep here in the office, were it not against
the rules and regulations."

Alf thanked him for his kindness and courtesy;
but the sampan men had aroused all his pride of
race and doggedness, and the problem could not be
solved that way. To sleep out the night on the stones
was an acknowledgment of defeat.

"The sampan men refuse to take me out?"

The lieutenant nodded.

"And you refuse to take me out?"

Again the lieutenant nodded.

"Well, then, it's not in the rules and regulations
that you can prevent my taking myself out?"

The lieutenant was perplexed. "There is no
boat," he said.

"That's not the question," Alf proclaimed hotly.
"If I take myself out, everybody's satisfied and no
harm done?"

"Yes; what you say is true," persisted the puzzled lieutenant. "But you cannot take yourself out."

"You just watch me," was the retort.

Down went Alf's cap on the office floor. Right
and left he kicked off his low-cut shoes. Trousers
and shirt followed.

"Remember," he said in ringing tones, "I, as a
citizen of the United States, shall hold you, the city
of Yokohama, and the government of Japan respon-
sible for those clothes. Good night."

He plunged through the doorway, scattering the astounded boatmen to either side, and ran out on the pier. But they quickly recovered and ran after him, shouting with glee at the new phase the situation had taken on. It was a night long remembered among the water-folk of Yokohama town. Straight to the end Alf ran, and, without pause, dived off cleanly and neatly into the water. He struck out with a lusty, single-overhand stroke till curiosity prompted him to halt for a moment. Out of the darkness, from where the pier should be, voices were calling to him.

He turned on his back, floated, and listened.

"All right! All right!" he could distinguish from the babel. "No pay now; pay bime by! Come back! Come back now; pay bime by!"

"No, thank you," he called back. "No pay at all. Good night."

Then he faced about in order to locate the *Annie Mine*. She was fully a mile away, and in the darkness it was no easy task to get her bearings. First, he settled upon a blaze of lights which he knew nothing but a man-of-war could make. That must be the United States war-ship *Lancaster*. Somewhere to the left and beyond should be the *Annie Mine*. But to the left he made out three lights close together. That could not be the schooner. For the moment he was confused. He rolled over on his back and shut his eyes, striving to construct a mental picture of the harbor as he had seen it in daytime. With a snort of satisfaction he rolled back again. The three lights evidently belonged to the big English tramp steamer. Therefore the schooner must lie somewhere between the three lights and the *Lancaster*. He gazed long and steadily, and there, very dim and low, but at the point he expected, burned a single light — the anchor-light of the *Annie Mine*.

And it was a fine swim under the starshine. The air was warm as the water, and the water as warm as tepid milk. The good salt taste of it was in his mouth, the tingling of it along his limbs; and the steady beat of his heart, heavy and strong, made him glad for living.

But beyond being glorious the swim was uneventful. On the right hand he passed the many-lighted *Lancaster*, on the left hand the English tramp, and ere long the *Annie Mine* loomed large above him. He grasped the hanging rope-ladder and drew himself noiselessly on deck. There was no one in sight. He saw a light in the galley, and knew that the captain's son, who kept the lonely anchor-watch, was making coffee. Alf went forward to the forecastle. The men were snoring in their bunks, and in that confined space the heat seemed to him insufferable. So he put on a thin cotton shirt and a pair of dungaree trousers, tucked blanket and pillow under his arm, and went up on deck and out on the forecastle-head.

Hardly had he begun to doze when he was roused by a boat coming alongside and hailing the anchor-watch. It was the police-boat, and to Alf it was given to enjoy the excited conversation that ensued. Yes, the captain's son recognized the clothes. They belonged to Alf Davis, one of the seamen.

What had happened? No; Alf Davis had not come aboard. He was ashore. He was not ashore? Then he must be drowned. Here both the lieutenant and the captain's son talked at the same time, and Alf could make out nothing. Then he heard them come forward and rouse out the crew. The crew grumbled sleepily and said that Alf Davis was not in the forecastle; whereupon the captain's son waxed indignant at the Yokohama police and their ways, and the lieutenant quoted rules and regulations in despairing accents.

Alf rose up from the forecastle-head and extended his hand, saying:

"I guess I'll take those clothes. Thank you for bringing them aboard so promptly."

"I don't see why he couldn't have brought you aboard inside of them," said the captain's son.

And the police lieutenant said nothing, though he turned the clothes over somewhat sheepishly to their rightful owner.

The next day, when Alf started to go ashore, he found himself surrounded by shouting and gesticulating, though very respectful, sampan men, all extraordinarily anxious to have him for a passenger. Nor did the one he selected say, "You pay now," when he entered his boat. When Alf prepared to step out on to the pier, he offered the man the customary ten sen. But the man drew himself up and shook his head.

"You all right," he said. "You no pay. You never no pay. You bully boy and all right."

And for the rest of the *Annie Mine's* stay in port, the sampan men refused money at Alf Davis's hand. Out of admiration for his pluck and independence, they had given him the freedom of the harbor.